Acknowlegements

My immense gratitude to Mr Mohammed Amin MBE,
Trustee of the National Muslim War Memorial Trust,
for his invaluable input and guidance.

I Remember ...

First Published in 2022 by
THE ISLAMIC FOUNDATION

Distributed by
KUBE PUBLISHING LTD
Tel +44 (0)1530 249230
E-mail: info@kubepublishing.com
Website: www.kubepublishing.com

Author: Maidah Ahmad
Illustrator: Kristina Swarner
Book design: Rebecca Wildman

A Cataloguing-in-Publication Data record for this book is available from the British Library

ISBN 978-0-86037-897-6

ISBN 978-0-86037-803-7 (e-book)

Printed in China

I Remember...

A recognition of Muslim loyalty and sacrifice in WW1

Maidah Ahmad

Illustrator: Kristina Swarner

Dear Great-grandpa, I remember you signed
up to fight in the Great War,
leaving behind your home and family.

Did your mum cry
when you left?

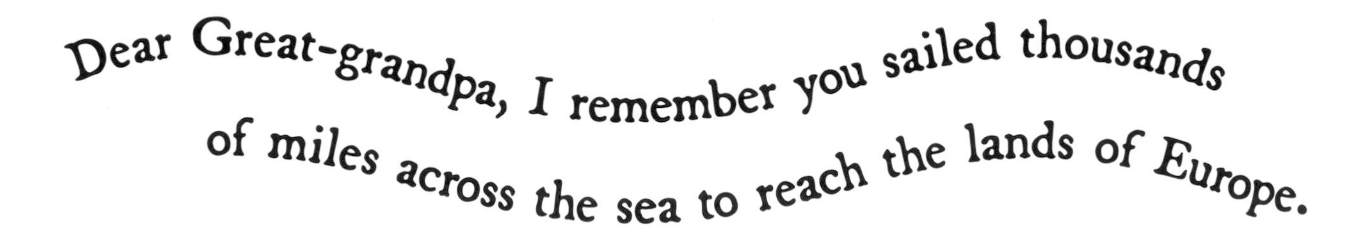

Dear Great-grandpa, I remember you sailed thousands of miles across the sea to reach the lands of Europe.

Did you get seasick?

Dear Great-grandpa, I remember how cold you were, far from the heat and warmth of India.

Did you drink tea to warm you up?

Dear Great-grandpa, I remember you fought alongside men who spoke an unfamiliar language.

Did you learn any English or French?

Dear Great-grandpa, I remember you lived in the trenches with soldiers who looked different from you.

Did they find your turban strange?

Dear Great-grandpa, I remember the blast of bombs and cries of soldiers kept you up all night.

Did you miss the sounds of your village?

Dear Great-grandpa, I remember
halal food was made for you.

Did you share your meals?

Dear Great-grandpa, I remember you used to keep fasts during Ramadan.

Did you eat dates for Iftar?

Dear Great-grandpa, I remember you learnt prayers to recite for the fallen.

Did you dream of
making it home?

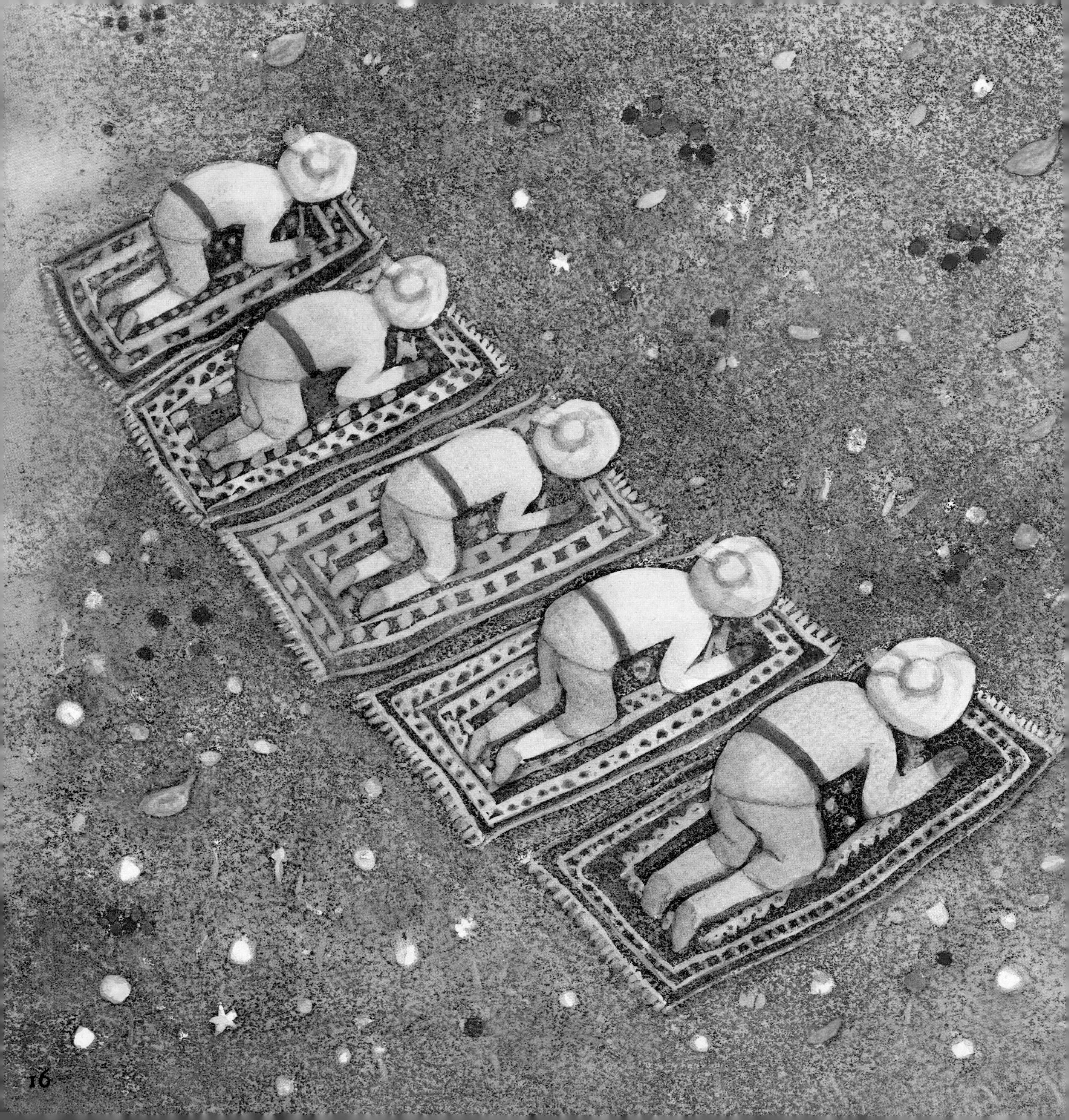

Dear Great-grandpa,
I remember you had to wait
for the fighting to pause before
you could pray.

Did you bring your
prayer mat?

Dear Great-grandpa, I remember you treated the prisoners of war with kindness and fed them when they were hungry.

Did you remain friends?

Dear Great-grandpa, I remember when you were injured, you applied traditional herbal medicines brought from back home.

Did your wounds heal quickly?

Dear Great-grandpa, I remember while you lay dying, the shahadah was recited in your ears to comfort you.

Dear Great-grandpa, I remember...

DID YOU KNOW?

- More than 2.5 million Muslim soldiers and labourers contributed to the Allied forces war effort.
- 1.3 million Indians served in WWI, at least 400,000 were Muslims.
- Over 50,000 Muslims served in the British Merchant Navy. 800,000 Muslims from North, East and West Africa served in the French Armed Forces.
- 1.3 million Muslims served in the Russian Army.
- 5,000 Muslims served in the American Forces.

Data from: National Muslim War Memorial Trust (muslimwarmemorial.org)

GLOSSARY

Halal: Permissible; used to refer to meat from permissible animals, slaughtered according to Islamic law.

Iftar: The meal after a fast.

Ramadan: The ninth month of the Islamic calendar; the month of fasting.

Shahadah: The testimony of faith.

Turban: A head covering for a man; made from a long piece of cloth wound tightly around the head.

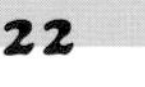

FUN FACTS

Three Muslims were awarded the Victoria Cross for their exceptional bravery and service during WWI: Khudadad Khan, Shahamad Khan and Mir Dast.

To cater to the different dietary and religious requirements of the British Indian army, they assigned specially trained cooks to every battalion. The religious composition of the battalion determined whether a Muslim, Sikh or Hindu cook was assigned.

To ensure they met religious requirements, sheep and goats were slaughtered on the spot, providing fresh halal meat to Muslim soldiers.

The Royal Pavilion in Brighton, UK, was used as a military hospital to treat the sick and wounded soldiers of the British Indian Army during World War One. Muslim soldiers were given space to say their daily prayers on the eastern grounds, which faced Makkah.

Princess Mary Gift Boxes were sent to all soldiers fighting overseas during WWI. The embossed brass tins contained tobacco, cigarettes, a pipe, a lighter, a Christmas card and a photograph of the Princess. Non-smokers received stationery inside their boxes, and Indian soldiers received spices and sweets inside theirs.

MORE INFORMATION:
Forgotten Heroes 14-19 Foundation
National Muslim War Memorial Trust

N
ONDON
1
2
7
5
2
6
1
3
4
Places to Visit